West Slide Story

By Doug Peterson
Illustrated by Michael Moore

BIG IDEA
BOOKS®

zonder**kidz**

ZONDERVAN.COM/
AUTHOR**TRACKER**

www.bigidea.com

The children's group
of Zondervan

www.zonderkidz.com

Library of Congress Cataloging-in-Publication Data

Peterson, Doug.
    West slide story : a lesson in making peace / by Doug Peterson.
        p. cm. -- (VeggieTown values ; bk. 7)
    Summary: After observing a dispute on the Veggie Town playground, Junior and
        Laura find themselves employing an unusual problem-solving technique to
        decide who will use the new equipment at West Slide Park.
    ISBN-13: 978-0-310-70742-4 (softcover)
    ISBN-10: 0-310-70742-0 (softcover)
    [1. Sharing--Fiction. 2. Conduct of life--Fiction. 3. Vegetables--Fiction.] I. Title. II.
        Series.
    PZ7.P44334Wes 2006
    [E]--dc22
                                                                        2005025258

Written by: Doug Peterson
Illustrated by: Michael Moore
Editor: Amy DeVries
Art direction & design: Karen Poth

Printed in Hong Kong

06 07 08 09 • 7 6 5 4 3 2 1

"Blessed are those who make peace.
They will be called sons of God."
(Matthew 5:9)

"No boys allowed," said Megan Radish. "Besides, we were here first."

"We called 'dibs,'" said Lenny Carrot. "So the boys get the jungle gym today!"
"We called 'double dibs'!" answered Megan. "So the girls get to play here all week!"
"You can't call double dibs!"
"Can too!"
"Cannot!"
"Can . . . !"
It was just another day on the VeggieTown playground.

The giant new jungle gym had monkey bars and slides and climbing tubes.
"It's amazing," the girls said. "It's our turn to use it."
"No, it's awesome," argued the boys. "And it's our turn to use it."

"It's big enough for everyone," Laura Carrot whispered to Junior Asparagus. Junior agreed. But they were afraid to point this out. Laura thought the girls would get mad. Junior feared the boys would say he was siding with the girls.

So they did nothing, and the arguing went on.

"Can!"

"Can't!"

"Can!"

Later that day, Junior and Laura went to the Treasure Trove Bookstore to get away from the bickering on the playground.

"The playground is no fun anymore," Laura complained as she smacked her bubblegum.

"I wish we could stop the fighting," said Junior.

"But you *can* do something," said Mr. O'Malley, owner of the bookstore. "All of God's children can be peacemakers. When you make peace, everyone wins. I've got just the book to prove it."

The old Irish potato hopped onto a rolling book cart and coasted down a long aisle. "You'll love this book. It's somewhere in the 'Give Peas a Chance' section, not far from my copy of *War and Peas*."

Mr. O'Malley tossed Junior a book called *West Slide Story*. Junior opened it to a picture of two groups of kids facing each other on a playground.

Suddenly, four giant words floated up from the book. Four simple words: Once Upon A Time . . .

The words swirled around Junior and Laura. They whirled and twirled and . . .

WHOOOOOOOOOOOOSH!

Junior and Laura tumbled **down**
      down
        down.

Clunk!

They landed smack-dab on a giant slide. They zipped down the twisting slide like a pair of rockets and landed right between two groups of kids.

A cucumber named Hairbrush yanked Junior into his group and said, "You're with us, not them, Daddy-O." The kids in the cucumber's group wore black leather jackets and looked like they had smeared grease in their hair. They were the "Greaseballs".

Laura started to follow Junior. A broccoli girl named Beehive stopped her.
"Where ya goin', sister?" said Beehive. She smacked her gum.
"I'm following my . . . uh . . . friend," squeaked Laura.

Beehive blew a huge bubble. "But you're chewing gum, so you're with us, not them. We're the Gumballs, and we don't hang out with Greaseballs."

"Oh . . . right." Laura stared at the ground and backed away.

All at once, the two groups started circling each other. They made the sound of fingers snapping—which seemed strange since none of them had fingers.
Snap! Snap! Snap! Snap!

"What's going on?" Junior asked Hairbrush.

"We're going to decide once and for all who gets to use the big slide here at West Slide Park," said Hairbrush. "Will it be the Greaseballs or the Gumballs?"

Junior glanced around. The slide looked plenty big enough for everyone. But Junior kept quiet.

Snap! Snap! Snap! Snap!

"So, how are you going to decide?" Junior asked.

"That's easy," said a gourd called Rebel Without a Comb. "We're going to hoop for it."

With that, everyone pulled out a hula hoop. They twirled the hoops around and around and around.

The Gumballs and Greaseballs gave Junior and Laura hoops too. "Twirl 'em," they said.

"Why?" Laura asked.

"This is a battle to the finish," Beehive answered. "Whoever keeps their hula hoop going the longest wins. If a Gumball wins, we get the slide. If a Greaseball wins, they get the slide."

But there was something the West Slide Park kids didn't know. Junior and Laura were champion hula-hoopers.

Ten minutes went by. Seven kids dropped out. But Junior and Laura kept going strong.

"Go, man, go!"

"Play it cool, cat!"

As time went on, the kids gave up, one by one. Finally, there were only two—Junior and Laura.

All of the kids formed a circle around them. Neither one showed any sign of tiring.

Beehive and her friends popped bubblegum in Junior's face. That didn't stop Junior. Hairbrush and his buddies squirted greasy hair stuff on the ground around Laura. But she didn't fall—or stop.

Junior and Laura thought the two groups should forget the contest and play together in peace. But they were too afraid to say anything.

One hour later, it seemed as if the contest would never end.
Both sides glared at each other. Junior and Laura didn't know what to do.

Then Junior remembered Mr. O'Malley's words: "All of God's children can be peacemakers."

Junior and Laura had to take action.

But did they have the courage?

Then the most incredible thing happened.
They stopped hula-hooping.
In stunned silence, everyone watched as Junior's and Laura's hula hoops came to a stop and hit the ground—at the exact same moment.

"Who won?" asked a baffled Rebel.

"Everyone wins!" exclaimed Junior.

"It's a tie!" said Laura. "And that means all of the kids get to use the slide."

"But . . . but . . . ," sputtered Hairbrush.

Beehive was so shocked, her bubblegum popped right in her own face.

"Let's go, Daddy-Os," Junior said. "We all slide!"

After a moment of shock, all the kids swarmed the giant slide. And to their amazement, they found that it was more fun to make peace than make trouble.

"Just call me Peacemaker," Hairbrush said. "That's my new nickname."

The kids ended the day with a sock-hop—a game in which they hopped over socks to the sound of music. And as they did, two giant words came slipping down the slide: **THE END**.

"It's time to go," said Laura sadly.

"Peace, sister," said Beehive with a smile.

With a final farewell, Junior and Laura slid back home and found themselves in the Treasure Trove Bookstore.

Mr. O'Malley was doing the hula hoop to the sound of Elvis music. What a scary sight.

"Did everything work out in *West Slide Story*?" asked the old potato.

"You bet," said Junior.

"And you were right," added Laura. "When you make peace, everyone wins."

"God was right," declared Mr. O'Malley. "Come on! Grab a hula hoop!"

Suddenly, Mr. O'Malley began to sing . . . off-key: "Tonight! Tonight! There won't be any fight. Tonight there will be peace all around!"

"Uh—we gotta get going," said Junior as he and Laura slipped out the door.

Junior and Laura headed straight for the VeggieTown playground. There they made peace between the girls and boys.

"It's been a long, crazy day," Laura said.

Junior yawned. "I think we need a little peas and quiet."